Roots and Wings

SABRINA GESE

WestBow Press books may be ordered through booksellers or by contacting:

WestBow Press
A Division of Thomas Nelson & Zondervan
1663 Liberty Drive
Bloomington, IN 47403
www.westbowpress.com
844-714-3454

www.sabrina-gese.com

ISBN: 979-8-3850-1930-4 (sc)
ISBN: 979-8-3850-1931-1 (hc)
ISBN: 979-8-3850-1932-8 (e)

Library of Congress Control Number: 2024903507

Print information available on the last page.

WestBow Press rev. date: 07/09/2024

WESTBOW
PRESS®
A DIVISION OF THOMAS NELSON
& ZONDERVAN

For Chris.
It has been a great privilege to share such a life with you.

A spot in the sky,
Her flight was the way.
She flew up so high,
Observing the lay.

The wind sang a song.
The currents declared.
A heavenly throng.
A vision they shared.

They held her aloft
For comfort and care.
A whisp'ring so soft,
A guide through the air.

And all through the day and all through the night,
She traveled, she rested, up again at first light.

Days later she spied
A tall, handsome tree.
Its branches were wide.
Its song was a plea.

"Come make me your home.
You'll be safe and warm.
My leaves are a dome
To keep you from harm."

5

She flew all around,
And when she alit,
She knew she had found
A right and well fit.

She loved its rough bark and impressive height,
Hopeful and awed by its presence and might.

The warm sun arose,
And when she could see,
A lone bird stood close
On her mighty tree.

He'd not planned to stay,
Was out for an eve.
A beam lit the way,
And he could not leave.

They made a fine pair.
She gave him a smile,
Then took to the air
And sped for a mile.

And chasing her up, they started a flight
That sealed a future, a promise so bright.

Around and around
The courtship went on,
From high up to ground,
A bond firmly drawn.

Working together,
They chose a fine place.
Sticks, moss and feathers
For their little space.

And after a while,
Four eggs appeared there,
A small speckled pile
That needed their care.

Day after day they spent
setting things right,
Gath'ring, preparing
for any new plight.

With each special hatch,
Their hearts filled with pride.
Young, free ones to latch
And for them to guide.

The days went by fast.
They grew more and more.
From first then to last,
They taught them to soar.

15

And when harsh wind blew,
When rain lashed and drenched,
Their home stood on cue,
Firm, stalwart, and quenched.

Through every bad storm that gave them a fright
Were strong wing and branch to help them sleep tight.

Too soon the day came
Their chicks were all grown.
And each had a name
And learned what was shown.

Before they could start
A life fresh and new,
A check of the heart
Was needed to view

The right and the true
To keep their paths straight,
A course to stick to
The way to their fate.

Down they all flitted till roots were in sight,
The two reminding to take care and fight.

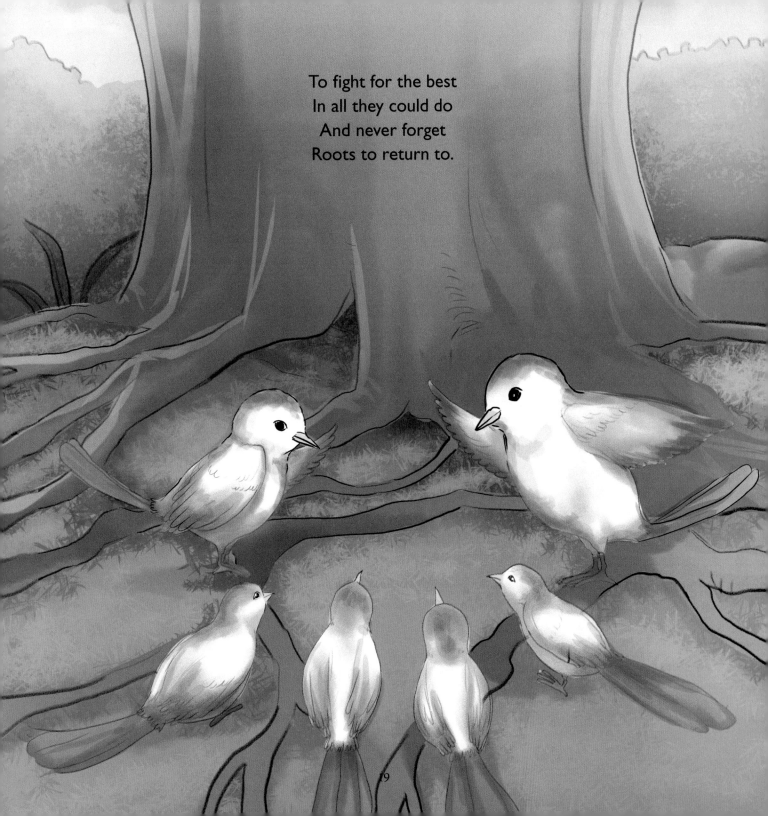

To fight for the best
In all they could do
And never forget
Roots to return to.

19

They'd been given wings
And much more besides,
Helpful and good things
To share far and wide.

Wherever life led
Through storm, woods, or vale,
Each way they should spread
The song of their tale.

Together they watched
each fly t'ward the light
And knew in their hearts
their future was bright.

21

Train up a child in the way he should go,
And when he is old he will not depart from it.
—Proverbs 22:6

Printed in the United States
by Baker & Taylor Publisher Services